THE PRINCE OF THE HEART OF GOLD

THE PRINCE OF THE HEART OF GOLD

ALDIVAN TORRES

Canary Of Joy

CONTENTS

1 1

CHAPTER 1

The Prince of the Heart of Gold
Aldivan Torres
The Prince of the Heart of Gold
Author: Aldivan Torres
© 2020- Aldivan Torres
All rights reserved.

This book, including all its parts, is protected by Copyright and cannot be reproduced without author's permission, or transferred.

Aldivan Torres, born in Brazil, is a consolidated writer in various genres. So far, the titles have been published in dozens of languages. Since his age, he's always been a lover of the art of writing, having consolidated a professional career from the second semester of 2013. Your mission is to conquer the heart of each of your readers. In addition to literature, its main amusements are music, travels, friends, family, and the pleasure of life itself. "For literature, equality, fraternity, justice, dignity, and honor of human being always" is your motto.

Book content

The prince of the heart of gold3

The Prince of the Heart of Gold 29

Prince of the Heart of Gold 313

Prince of the Heart of Gold 416

PRINCE OF THE HEART OF GOLD 520

Prince of the Heart of Gold 623

The prince of the heart of gold

Prince Zaci

What's going on, Taú? Where are we?

Taú

We've been kidnapped and arrested, Zaci. Bad luck has come for us.

Zaci

What's going to happen now? Where are we going?

Taú

Looks like they're taking us to the new continent.

Zaci

My God. I don't like this at all. I didn't want to leave my country. Furthermore, I have a kingdom to rule and a woman to love. What will become of my people in South Sudan?

Taú

I didn't want to leave there either. But being with you in this situation gives me strength. We will unite and try to survive this chaos.

Zaci

True. Thanks for the support. I don't know what I'd do without you. My best friend since childhood.

Taú

No need to thank me. I also need your support. I hope he'll protect us.

Zaci

Let him hear you.

Captain

Cut the chatter and get to work, niggers. Wash the ship out.

Taú

We'll be right there, sir.

Washing the ship

Female

My God. How cruel of you! This job is very hard.

Zaci

Don't you worry, lady. We're fine. What's your name?

Female

Sabrina and you?

Zaci

Zaci. Nice to meet you.

Taú

My name is Taú. We're used to hard work. We will resist because our will for freedom is greater than anything.

Female

But this is unfair. God created free men. Everyone, regardless of race, deserves to be respected.

Zaci

This is a world of illusion. Financial interests come first. But I am aware that for God we are equal.

Taú

We can only ask for strength so that we can

withstand all adversity. We are warriors, and we will not give up easily.

Female

Very interesting. I wanted to know your story. Could you tell me?

Zaci

I'm king in South Sudan. I lived in a palace surrounded by servants together with my wife. Foreigners invaded our territory, raped and killed my wife. Then they kidnapped us. That's why we're here.

Taú

I'm an aide to the king and his best childhood friend. Together, we were happy in Africa. Fate has taken everything from us. Now we have to fight.

Female

Well, then fight back. You can count on me for whatever you need.

Zaci

Thank you very much, ma'am. Now go away before they find us here.

Female

All right. Good job.

Party at night

Captain

Dance for us, niggers. We want to rejoice.

Black's dance

Captain

I didn't like the dance. You didn't feel like it. You will be punished.

Scenes of torture-beating blacks.

Afterward

Zaci

Where are we?

Taú

I'm glad you woke up. We suffered hours subservient to those bastards. They beat us till we were our cold.

Zaci

Damned! Bastards! What hatred of them.

Taú

Calm. We have nothing to gain by this affront. We'll just have to go through with it. When we get to the new continent, we can think of an escape route.

Zaci

If we survive, right? The way things are going, it's going to be very complicated.

Taú

Everything is possible for those who believe in God.

Sabrina

I came, my loves, and brought food. You need to stay strong.

Zaci

Thank you, Sabrina, thank you. We really needed it.

Sabrina

It was no big deal. I promised I'd help. I love to participate in good causes.

Taú

Still, we're very grateful. You're an angel in our lives.

Sabrina

Just consider me a servant of God. It's a long road. I will be with you at all times.

Zaci

May God bless you.

In the new land

captain

We arrived in Mimoso. This is the end for you niggers. I sold you to a farmer. You will be his slaves.

Zaci

What a downfall for someone who was once a king! But this is how it should be. You will still pay for it, Captain!

Captain

You're in no position to threaten! Be happy to be alive. I could have done something worse.

Taú

But you didn't do it to avoid injury. We're just commodities to you. Now that we are human beings with values. That's something you'll never understand.

Captain

That's enough! The farmer's already on his way! Thank God I'm rid of you once and for all.

BIG HOUSE

Aluízio

Daughter, some blacks have just arrived from the capital. They go work the farm. You want to go with me to see them?

Catherine

Of course, Father. I need new slaves in the big house. I will choose personally.

In the corral

Catherine

They're beautiful, Father. Would you grant me a wish?

Aluízio

Whatever you want, daughter.

Catherine

I want them working for me in my personal enclosure. I miss a male presence around me.

Aluízio

All right, my daughter. They're at your disposal.

Catherine

All right, black people. What are their names?

Zaci

My name is Zaci. I'm at your service, miss.

Tau

My name is Taú. I'm happy to serve you. Nothing bad is going to happen to you. You can trust us.

Catherine

I like you guys. I saved you the hard work. All you have to do is keep up and do housework because I'm not good at it.

Taú

I'm an excellent cook and Zaci is a great fighter. You couldn't be in better hands.

Catherine

I really like that information. I hope you'll be happy here. Furthermore, I know it's hard being a slave in a distant country, but that's how the law works. I sympathize with the slave cause.

Zaci

You seem like an excellent person. I've taken a liking to you.

Taú

I liked her once, too. Very polite, intelligent and nice. Quite humble for a landowner.

Catherine

Thank you, both very much. I'm an evolved woman. I think we're going to get along just fine.

The Prince of the Heart of Gold 2

In the lady's room

Catherine

You've been here for days and I don't know anything about you. I'd like to know more of your history. Could you tell me?

Zaci

I was king in South Sudan. I lived a pompous and joyful life. Furthermore, I was served by millions, and my government wisely directed them all.

They were memorable and virtuous times until the worst happened. We were robbed and kidnapped. They brought us here.

Taú

I was his aide. I participated in the government with several projects. We were respected and happy. We don't have anything today.

Catherine

Don't talk like that. It causes me severe sadness. I think slavery is completely unfair. That's why I wanted to protect them. More than servants, you will be my friends and confidants. Nothing will be lacking for you. I think freedom is not so far away. There are several social movements in defense of the freedom of blacks in the country. Society has been evolving gradually and injustices will be corrected.

Zaci

I hope so, miss. After all these sad facts, you were a good thing that happened to us. It's what gives us hope for a better and fairer future. You look like my wife. I was pleased with my wife in Africa. We had many happy times. We used to travel and work together. Furthermore, we were totally connected. Leaving her has brought me much sadness. I'm not over this trauma yet. It was more than ten years of lasting coexistence. Anyway, finding you helps us feel better.

Taú

I also had a wife and kids. It brings us great sadness. Your presence and support are important immediately. We need a lot of strength to face our destiny. Many of our brothers have died. They died in the slave quarters, humiliated and tortured. It's decades of white man humiliation and contempt. It's not fair to work to enrich others. Furthermore, it's not fair to live out other people's dreams. We have our individuality and dreams. We demand our rights as a human being that we are. Furthermore, we demand our freedom and individuality. Without it, we'll never be happy.

Catherine

I understand. You can count on me. I'm at your disposal. We've been friends ever since. We will be complicit in work and in life. Furthermore, we will be a team searching for happiness, freedom, and fulfillment. I have a lot of faith in the future. I hope that our work together will bear fruit. Let's not give up on achieving our dreams. Although the obstacles are gigantic, we can face them with a lot of grit, strength, and faith. I believe in our potential and in solving ideas. We can build something beneficial together. Well, that's what I had to say. I need to be alone. Go take care of the horses.

Zaci

All right, young lady.

Taú

We're going. Stay with God.

Catherine

I'm reflecting a little. What a pain those two have been through. They live entirely different stories nowadays. I understand their concern and their suffering. They're in a strange country like slaves. This is something very painful. I'll be their protector. Nothing bad is going to happen to you two. I feel good in their company. They look like two princes to me. One of them has a heart of gold. He's kind and polite and helpful. A great man who's going through a bad time. I need to help both of you find happiness in this distant land. It's a mission I have. I have no interest in that. I want to see you both happy. Contributing to this will make me pleased. I've been thinking about my noble trajectory. I was born into a rich family, but I was always attentive to the needs of the poor. We are equal human beings. I am the sister of blacks, whites, Indians or any minority. We are children of the same God.

Dine

Aluízio

Good night, my child. How are the employees working on the farm?

Catherine

They are doing very well. I guided the slaves and each one went to do his task. With my coordination, profits have increased. We are living in a period of financial calm. This allows us to make some extravagances. I want new clothes and shoes. I want good food and good leisure. We need to take advantage of the fruits of our labor.

Aluízio

I agree. But we also need to save a little money. It's a safe way to avoid the crisis. There are already many rumors that slavery will soon be over. It totally hurts us.

Catherine

I don't think that's entirely bad, Dad. We can continue with the same employees on fairer terms. It would be extremely beneficial for our blacks.

We're already wealthy and rewarding the job would be great. In evolved societies, there is no slavery.

Aluízio

You're a great daughter but a lousy visionary. The more profit for us, the better. I prefer things the way they are. It's more comfortable for us.

Catherine

I don't agree, but I respect your opinion. I wanted a fairer world.

Aluízio

How are your servants treating you?

Catherine

Okay. I found out that one of them was a king in Africa. Who knew one of our slaves was once a king. That sounds like a fantasy story.

Aluízio

This is really wonderful. But be careful with them. We have to avoid closer contact. We each have our place.

Catherine

I know that, Dad. But they seem pretty peaceful to me. They treat me very well. I believe I am not in great danger.

Aluízio

Good. Anything, just let me know.

Prince of the Heart of Gold 3

Late in the crop

Catherine

Good afternoon, my loves. I came to check on the farm work and see how they're doing. I think it must be exhausting and tedious this work.

Taú

We're used to it, miss. Work dignifies the man. I think our contribution will be important for the growth of the country's economy. Besides, even though we're slaves, it's good to feel useful.

Zaci

We're very well, young lady. This is not an appropriate place for people of your level. You should be resting at the farm. The strong sun can hurt your skin.

Catherine

I was bored at the farm. I like to interact, talk and see people. Everything for me is a matter of reflection, planning, and action.

Zaci

I get it. I sympathize with you. You're also gorgeous and charismatic.

Catherine

I appreciate your kindness. It's good to feel

beautiful. A compliment from a prince is critical to me. Every day I feel happier beside you. You can count on my help. I'll be your protector.

Taú

We really appreciate it. We have reason to keep dreaming of better days. Furthermore, we will continue to fight for the slave cause. There's a lot of movement in the country on that.

Catherine

You have my support. I just need a law to set them free. We all have that right.

Zaci

I agree. It's like the saying goes, everything happens at the right time. Let's work on our goals that victory will come.

In the pond

Zaci

It was a great idea to come here after a long day of work. Thanks for the opportunity, ma'am.

Taú

I love these leisure moments. We did that a lot in Africa. Just thinking about how much I miss you.

Catherine

No need to thank me. It's a great opportunity

for distraction. You deserve it for your dedication to the job. We can get to know each other better, too.

Zaci

I'll start. I'm a mature, hardworking, honest man. Furthermore, I have royal blood and peasant soul. Everything I do is for the love of my neighbor. We are facing an unjust society in its rules and values. I feel obliged to fight it with all my strength. I want to be remembered for my character and determination.

Taú

I'm a good servant. Furthermore, I carry out my duties. I'm also a great companion and friend. My friends praise me for my loyalty. And you? Who are you, miss?

Catherine

I was born into a rich family. The good financial situation allowed me to study and own my life very early. But regardless, I learned from life. I know that the reality of most people is different from my situation. I have a special appreciation for wronged minorities. Furthermore, I like to associate with noble causes. I want society to evolve and have more equality between human beings. We are all equal before God. As for the personal aspect, I'm a sweet, polite, intelligent maiden. I have good habits and values. I must confess, I'm passionate about men, especially blacks.

Zaci

Very well! I love women of any color. But I know I am of another level. I respect my bosses.

Catherine

I can't believe this. You're a prince, remember? Your level is even higher than mine.

Zaci

But now I'm just a simple slave. I don't want to get you in trouble, but I like you.

Taú

I support both of you. You make a beautiful couple. You can count on my protection. No one will know.

Zaci

So, you want to be my girlfriend, Catherine?

Catherine

I want. I liked you from the beginning. Furthermore, I'm not prejudiced because I'm an educated woman. We're going to be together. I've always sought the love of my life. Now that I've found it, I won't lose it. Let's make a beautiful story.

Zaci

I promise I'll make you happy. With discretion, we build a perfect relationship. When the time comes, we'll know how to act. I just know I want to have you as my wife. Even against everyone, I will fight for that love.

Catherine

I, too, will fight for that love. We are free and have the capacity to love. I don't care about rules. I just want to live and be happy.

Taú

Congratulations to the couple. May that love last forever. Love really is worth it. These are important moments in our lives that we must not miss. Let's put shame aside and enjoy what life offers us. I already have a girlfriend. My king was missing his love. I wish you all the happiness in the world. No one can separate you because I realize you truly love each other. Like I said, I'm here for you. I will be your accomplice at all times. You deserve to be happy.

Prince of the Heart of Gold 4

Big house

Zaci

Your father's out of town. This is a great chance for us to escape.

Catherine

Where are we going, love?

Taú

Let's go to the quilombo. Our black brothers are waiting for us.

Forest

Zaci

Why did you accept my offer? It's too risky for a young maiden to run away from home. I have nothing to offer you.

Catherine

Because I love you and I like intense adventures. Rich life never appealed to me. I've always felt in a bad position. I'll settle for little. All you need is love and freedom.

Taú

You are really brave. But how will your father react?

Catherine

I left a letter explaining everything. My father would never condemn me. He loves me.

Zaci

But he wouldn't accept me as your husband. I must guard against any reprisals. I don't regret my act. Furthermore, I wanted to be free in its full expression.

Catherine

I support you, my love. I'll be wherever you are.

On the farm

farmer

My daughter ran off with those two black guys. What wrong have I done, my God? I raised a daughter with such zeal to make her a nigger's wife.

Governess

I understand your pain, Baron. But it was her choice. We need to respect that.

Farmer

I won't respect it. I want my daughter back. Furthermore, I'll report you to the authorities. I'll find them even in hell.

Delegate

What is it, Baron? What's all the shouting about?

Farmer

I'm glad you came. Two black men took my daughter to the quilombo. This is a kidnapping. We need to help my daughter.

Delegate

Are you sure she was kidnapped? Going after them is reckless. They know how to defend themselves.

Farmer

I don't want to know! Ask the governor to help you send in the troops. Let's show these niggers whose boss.

Delegate

All right! I'll do what I can.

Making

Do the impossible thing! I want satisfactory results or else you'll lose your job.

Delegate

All right, Baron, all right! I promise you'll get the results.

In the quilombo

Zaci

Are you all, right? How do you feel?

Catherine

Happy and worried. I don't want you to suffer because of me. You should have left me behind. It's the only way you'd have a better chance of escape.

Zaci

I had no way out. Living as a slave is very outrageous to me. I had to take a chance. I have royal blood. Furthermore, I deserve the hope of freedom and love.

Catherine

I believe I have a share of responsibility for that. What happens after that? They'll be looking for us by now. I imagine they'll want to find us at any cost. They might arrest you, but I'm going with them. I will not open this love even in the face of death.

Zaci

I never thought I'd find a white woman so determined. You remind me of my wife from Africa. I believe that too is love. Love is something totally without control and inexplicable. I like that feeling. I believe in his power to produce miracles because God Himself is love. We are the fruit of this love that surpasses reincarnations. I'm a big believer in fate. I believe we are spirits linked to other reincarnations. At the right moment, we found ourselves in an unfavorable situation in this life and the pain united us. Pain gives us courage and strength. Hope and faith transform relationships. Actions show who we are and what we desire. We are the union of desires and struggles. Creator's apprentices in a world of atonement and trials. Here we are, waiting for things to happen.

Catherine

True! We're ready for anything. Our strength strengthens and comforts us. We'll wait for our executioners with our heads held high. We will face our destiny with courage. Death is nothing compared to our wildest dreams. You have to take risks being happy.

Zaci

Nothing will happen to you. You can rest easy. Let our enemies come in pursuit. I'm not going up against them. I really wish I had a reason to talk to your father. Our escape was a pretext. I couldn't keep it a secret my whole life. We need to lose our fear and face our opponents. I see rumors that slavery is ending. All that remains is to sign the law, which could happen in the next few days. Through legal channels, we want our right as citizens.

Taú

Calm down your hearts. We have a great God on our side. Everything in our life is written. I'm sure you wrote a beautiful story for yourselves. Your love is true. You have a right to be together.

I will support and protect you both. I'm a trained warrior. We're stronger than the government.

PRINCE OF THE HEART OF GOLD 5

ZACI

At last, you have arrived. My wife and I were waiting. We need to talk urgently.

Baron

You've done me a great disservice. You kidnapped my daughter without explanation. This can't go on like this. You'll have to pay for your mistakes.

Catherine

That's not true, Dad. I came of my own free will. You have to understand that we love each other, and we need to be together.

Taú

I am a witness. Your daughter wasn't forced to do anything. We just wanted to be entitled to our space. We also need the freedom that every human being deserves.

Baron

I just want my daughter back and that delinquent locked up. Do your duty, general.

THE PRINCE OF THE HEART OF GOLD - 27

General

Right away, Baron, immediately. I love doing justice. Don't fight back, nigga. It would be better to accept the situation peacefully.

Zaci

I'm coming with you. Set the others free. Do not hurt anyone.

Catherine

I will go with you and fight for justice. It's going to be okay, baby.

In the big house

Baron

Now it's our turn to talk. What madness is this, my daughter? With that attitude, we were mocked by the whole region. Haven't you thought about the shame you'd provoke? My family is demoralized.

Catherine

I didn't demoralize my family. I just wanted to take over my relationship. Furthermore, I don't think it's fair for a hypocritical society to have the power to dictate my fate. I want the chance to have a good time and be happy. I support freedom for all human beings because that is how God created us. It won't be you or anyone else who keeps me from being happy. Not even death can stop true love. You're the one who let me down, Dad. I expected your support and understanding at a difficult time like this. I was hoping you'd understand my reasons for acting like this. Furthermore, I was hoping you'd drop the social conventions and accept me. That's a big disappointment to me, a lot bigger than yours. Don't you understand that you are losing the only love of your life for petty attitudes? Who's going to take care of you when you're older? Who's been with you your whole life without an explanation? I expected more from you. I'm your only daughter. If I ran away, it's because I had no choice. I'm not happy in my personal life. I didn't ask to be born rich or to be an explorer. Furthermore, I want to be a woman. My life project is getting married and having kids. I found it in the Prince of the Heart of Gold, my true love. Respect my choice and release my love.

Baron

Looks like you didn't learn anything. You don't know the real dimension of this problem. We're arrested for reason, child. It's a disgrace to marry a black man because he's not on your social level. Besides, he's a slave. Don't you understand that there is an insurmountable abyss between you?

Catherine

He's not my social level. He's on a higher level. Furthermore, he was a prince in his country. He has noble lineage. But regardless, we love each other. Nothing can change that.

Taú

Good afternoon to you all. I come with great news. Princess Elizabeth has just signed into law. From now on, all slaves are free. There's no reason to keep Zaci locked up. We will demand your freedom.

Baron

All right, you win. You can go after him. But you don't have my blessing. I don't want to know any more about you. The dream ended here. I don't care how old I am. I'm still wealthy, and I can find a good woman. You can leave immediately.

Taú

You don't know the mistake you're making. Your daughter is a wonderful person, and she doesn't deserve this. Old cranky and ignorant. You're going to suffer a lot.

Catherine

We will respect your decision. I'm not going to die because of your contempt, Dad. I'm going to leave my happy life with my husband. Furthermore, I'm going to live my life with faith in God. I can lose everything in my life, except my trust in God. I can only wish you good luck.

Police station

Taú

We've come for you, sparring partner. The bondage is over. Now we are all equal and free.

Zaci

What a wonderful gift of life! You mean we can finally be happy? This is almost unbelievable.

Catherine

Believe me, my love. It's the honest truth. From here we go to the quilombo. We will begin a new life without further persecution. Life has given us a chance to be happy. We need to take advantage of this.

Zaci

True. At this moment, I imagine the suffering of all my murdered brothers. This is our achievement. I didn't think I was going to be happy in love either. But a big surprise comes along. I am completely happy. Thank God for that.

Taú

Thank our great God. Let's start making plans for the future. The challenge begins now.

Prince of the Heart of Gold 6

Lying in bed

Baron

Please, I need help. I suffer many pains and loneliness. I don't feel well. Stay with me. I'll give you a lot of money. I'm a wealthy man and I can make your dreams come true. Now, don't be shy. You can come closer. I need warmth. I need to feel important. Furthermore, I want to have a reason to live and dream. After all these years, I think I deserve it. I've always been fair to my employees. I've always been honest in my business. Then I deserve a break. I deserve a human refuge.

Maid

Don't make me laugh. You've always been a crooked bastard. You enslaved the blacks and drove his daughter out of here. Furthermore, you deserve to suffer so much to pay for your sins. You won't get my help. You will suffer slowly. Not even the salary you pay right. I'm not your daughter! If you wanted peace, you would have accepted your daughter. You're a prejudiced, ignorant old man. You think everything revolves around you. Furthermore, you're nothing but a nasty little worm. Take this moment of pain and think of all the harm you've done. Repent of your mistakes and try to be a better human being. Suffering energizes the soul. Pray and ask for protection from your saints. Your end is near. The sad saga of the Baron of Mimoso.

Baron

I am in dismay! I regret what I did to my daughter. Furthermore, I was a bully to her, and now I'm alone. I thought I'd be healthy for the rest of my life. But we are mortal. We are fragile beings who should not be proud. I hope that suffering releases my soul. I want to have a chance at reconciliation with the creator. When we don't learn in love, we learn in pain. I found that out too late.

Maid

I'm glad you thought it over. I'll ask for your soul. This disease of yours is hopeless. His death is inevitable. But if it served to reconcile him to God, it was a good opportunity. May God have mercy on you.

Quilombo

Catherine

How do you analyze our relationship?

Zaci

It was a gift in this world. When I had no hope of being happy, you showed up. When I was kidnapped in Africa, my world collapsed. My heart just overflowed with anger, anguish, and indignation. All I could think about was the disappointment in life. Many times, I reflected and wept with my misfortunes. I felt totally alone and desperate. I felt like nothing. But then I met you. I fell in love with you. I forgot my past of anguish and I rose again. Furthermore, I had the courage to face my worst enemies and I became a respected, free and happy man. I consider our relationship to be highly positive. We respect each other and love each other very much. Each of us has our freedom to make our own decisions. I feel pleased. And you? How do you feel?

Catherine

I feel like an accomplished woman. I transformed my concepts and revived my hopes. Furthermore, I opened myself up to destiny and found myself as a person. I opened my world view with new possibilities. Today I am a woman transformed by God and by life. Today I understand every aspect of humanity. I want to look for new things and experience different situations. I've learned it's living you learn. Furthermore, I understood that everything in the world has its time and place. I understand that we have to seize opportunities because they are unique opportunities. We have to try to find love without too many expectations. We need to forgive others and correct our mistakes. Furthermore, we need to persist in our dreams and make new plans. We need to believe in our ability even in the face of great obstacles. We need to be worth every moment.

Taú

I'm happy for both of you. I'm a witness to your love. Furthermore, I followed this path from the beginning and I can say that this love is true. We need more examples like this in our world. We need to believe in love even when it escapes us. Some things we should highlight: Faith, courage, determination, patience, union, and love. The greatest of them is love. Stay in that mood. You have everything to build a beautiful trajectory beyond prejudice. You are victorious because you believe in your project. Stay determined at all times.

I will always be with you for your protection. I thank this country that welcomed us with open arms. Furthermore, I already consider myself Brazilian and am enthusiastic about the nation. Let's make the nation grow and develop. We have great potential. We need to show the world what Brazil has. You are an example of a couple that has worked. Let this continue from generation to generation.

End

www.ingramcontent.com/pod-product-compliance
Lightning Source LLC
LaVergne TN
LVHW021049100526
838202LV00079B/5378